Dear Parent:
Your child's love of reading starts here!

Every child learns to read in a different way and at his or her own speed. Some go back and forth between reading levels and read favorite books again and again. Others read through each level in order. You can help your young reader improve and become more confident by encouraging his or her own interests and abilities. From books your child reads with you to the first books he or she reads alone, there are I Can Read Books for every stage of reading:

SHARED READING
Basic language, word repetition, and whimsical illustrations, ideal for sharing with your emergent reader

BEGINNING READING
Short sentences, familiar words, and simple concepts for children eager to read on their own

READING WITH HELP
Engaging stories, longer sentences, and language play for developing readers

READING ALONE
Complex plots, challenging vocabulary, and high-interest topics for the independent reader

ADVANCED READING
Short paragraphs, chapters, and exciting themes for the perfect bridge to chapter books

I Can Read Books have introduced children to the joy of reading since 1957. Featuring award-winning authors and illustrators and a fabulous cast of beloved characters, I Can Read Books set the standard for beginning readers.

A lifetime of discovery begins with the magical words "I Can Read!"

Visit www.icanread.com for information
on enriching your child's reading experience.

ISBN 978-0-545-43363-1

12 11 10 9 8 7 6 5 4 3 2 1   12 13 14 15 16/0

Printed in the U.S.A.   40

First Scholastic printing, November 2011

Typography by Joe Merkel

I Can Read!™

BEGINNING
1
READING

Dixie

Loves School Pet Day

story by Grace Gilman
pictures by Sarah McConnell
colors by Joe Merkel

SCHOLASTIC INC.
New York Toronto London Auckland
Sydney Mexico City New Delhi Hong Kong

Today was an important day.

Dixie was going to school

with Emma.

"Come on, Dixie," said Emma.

"I don't want to be late

for Pet Day!"

Dixie yipped.

She yapped.

Dixie didn't want

to be late either.

Dixie trotted by Emma's side
all the way to school.
"You must be good today," said Emma.
"No howling or barking."

Dixie wanted to do as Emma said.

She would try her very best.

But it was hard!

"Dixie!" called Emma

when Dixie ran after a chipmunk.

Emma brought Dixie

to her classroom.

Dixie had never seen

so many animals all at once!

There were hamsters

and turtles

and kittens

and lizards.

"It's a zoo in here!" Emma laughed.

"It's time for Pet Day to begin,"
said Emma's teacher.
"Would anyone like to bring
his or her pet
to the front of the class?"

Matt brought his goldfish.

Dixie wagged her tail.

Thump, thump, thump!

"Shhh," said Emma.

Anna showed the class

her ant farm.

Dixie let out a little yelp.

"Shhh," said Emma.

Jason showed off

his pet frog.

"*Arrooooooooo!*"

Dixie howled happily.

"Shhh!" said Emma.

"Emma, it looks like your pet

has something to say,"

said Emma's teacher.

"This is Dixie," said Emma.

"She loves all animals,

and she wants everyone to know that!"

Dixie yipped and yapped.

She agreed.

"Now let's walk around the room
and meet all the other pets,"
said the teacher.
Emma saw a girl she didn't know
very well.

The girl had a big cage on her desk with two small birds inside.

"Hi," Emma said.

"I'm Emma. I like your birds."

"Thanks," said the girl.

"I'm Amy.

I just moved here.

And these are Nate and Kate.

How old is your dog?" asked Amy.

Emma told Amy all about Dixie.

"Dixie is so cute," said Amy.

"Look at how she's making friends

with Nate and Kate."

Emma and Amy laughed.

Dixie was watching the birds.

Whenever Nate and Kate chirped,

Dixie wagged her tail.

Dixie wanted to get a closer look.

She bumped the bird cage

with her nose.

The cage door flew open.

Nate and Kate flew out!

"Oh no!" said Amy.

"Dixie!" yelled Emma.

"What did you do?"

Everyone tried to catch the birds.

Emma closed all the windows.

Amy closed the doors.

The teacher tried to catch the birds

with a butterfly net.

But Nate and Kate kept flying

all around the room!

"This is awful, Dixie," said Emma.

Dixie watched.

She felt very bad.

Dixie let out a sad little yelp

to let Amy know she was sorry.

Just then,

Nate and Kate swooped down.

They landed right on top of Dixie!

Dixie trotted carefully
back to the bird cage.
Nate and Kate didn't even try
to fly off her back.

Dixie yipped.

She yapped.

Nate and Kate chirped and cooed.

"Dixie saved the day!" said Amy.

"Looks like Dixie made
some new friends," said Emma.

"Yes," said Amy.

"And so did I!"